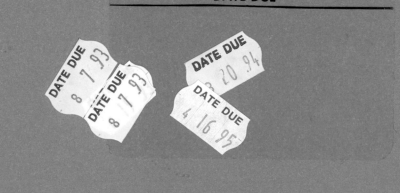

JAMES STEVENSON

DON'T YOU KNOW THERE'S A WAR ON?

Greenwillow Books, New York

Watercolor paintings were used for the full-color art.
The text type is ITC Bookman.
Copyright © 1992 by James Stevenson
All rights reserved. No part of this book
may be reproduced or utilized in any form
or by any means, electronic or mechanical,
including photocopying, recording or by
any information storage and retrieval
system, without permission in writing
from the Publisher, Greenwillow Books,
a division of William Morrow & Company, Inc.,
1350 Avenue of the Americas, New York, NY 10019.

Printed in Hong Kong by South China Printing Company (1988) Ltd.
First Edition   10 9 8 7 6 5 4 3 2 1

Library of Congress Cataloging-in-Publication Data
Stevenson, James (date)
Don't you know there's a war on? / by James Stevenson.
p.   cm.
Summary: The author recalls his efforts to win
the Second World War, including planting a victory
garden, collecting tinfoil, and looking for spies.
ISBN 0-688-11383-4 (trade). ISBN 0-688-11384-2 (lib.)
1. Stevenson, James (date).
Biography—Youth—Juvenile literature.
2. World War, 1939–1945—Personal narratives,
American—Juvenile literature.
3. Authors, American—20th century—
Biography—Juvenile literature.
4. Illustrators—United States—
Biography—Juvenile literature.
[1. Stevenson, James (date).   2. Authors, American.
3. Illustrators.   4. World War, 1939–1945—United States.] I. Title.
PZ7.S84748Do   1992   91-31461   CIP   AC

For Peter

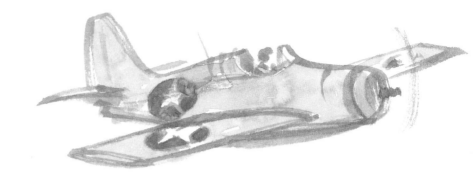

In 1942
there was a war.

My brother
went into
the navy.

I stayed home
with my father
and mother.

People kept saying, "Don't you know there's a war on?"

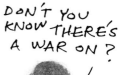

I tried to help win the war,

I collected
tinfoil
and rolled it
into a ball.

I saved
tin cans.

I bought war stamps.

I pulled down the shades
at night so the enemy
wouldn't see our lights.

Some food was rationed.
We planted a "victory garden"
and grew a lot of kale.

Nobody liked kale.
It tasted awful.

People got stickers for their windshields,
telling how much gas they were allowed.

Most people got
an "A" sticker,
which meant just a little gas.

If you got any
other sticker,
people wondered
how you got it.

Mr. Halstead
was the
air raid
warden.

He wore an official armband
and carried a flashlight.
He went around at night making sure
all the houses were blacked out.

Sometimes you could hear him making his rounds.

ATTENTION! THIS IS THE
AIR RAID WARDEN!

THE AIR RAID
WARDEN.

TURN OFF THAT
LIGHT.

THE ONE
UPSTAIRS.

OH, NEVER MIND.

WHO?

OH, IS THAT YOU,
HALSTEAD?

WHAT LIGHT?

WHERE? ON THE STAIRS?
THEN I WON'T BE ABLE
TO SEE A THING.

We were warned that spies called saboteurs
might sneak ashore from submarines
and blow things up.

They probably wanted to
blow up the power plant
and the railroad bridge.

I hoped they might get
Howard J. Davis Elementary School
by mistake.

We kept an eye on old Mr. Schmidt.
We thought he might be a spy.

We followed
him home.

We had to learn the shapes
of friendly and enemy planes.
It wasn't too easy.

FRIENDLY   ENEMY

FRIENDLY   ENEMY

When it got dark, my friends and I
watched the sky for enemy planes.

My friends talked about what they'd do in the war.

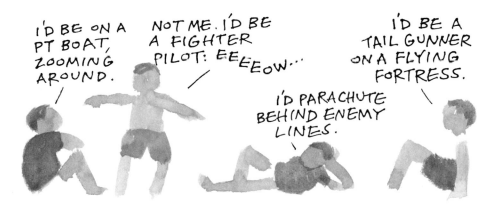

Nobody realized how brave
I would be if they just
allowed me to join the marines.

Sidney had a map of the world.
He stuck pins in it to show where
the fighting was.
If you said, "Where's Guadalcanal?"
Sidney would say, "Don't you know
anything?"

Sidney knew what all the medals
were for, too.

WHAT'S THIS
ONE, SID?

THE LEGION
OF MERIT,
OF COURSE.

Molly and David and I put out a weekly
one-page paper called *The Blackout*.

It told about who was
in the war ("David Grey's
Uncle George is a corporal
at Ft. Dix, N.J."),
but we didn't
give away any secrets.

We printed items about where people
could donate blood, and recipes that
included Spam and kale.

One day my father said,
"Let's go for a walk."
It was fun.
We didn't go for walks
together very often.

Then he told me he was going
to go away to join the army.
I started to cry.
My father told me to be brave.

"I want you to take care
of your mother," he said.

My father went away to the army on a train.

I walked around the house, looking at what my father had left behind. . . .

HIS BUREAU

HIS DESK

HIS CLOSET WITH
THE CLOTHES
HE WOULDN'T NEED

HIS BRIEFCASE

In his bathroom there was

NO SHAVING
BRUSH

NO
RAZOR

NO
TOOTHBRUSH

NO CAN OF
TOOTH POWDER

I kept a picture of my father in my room.
If I wished hard enough, he wouldn't get killed.

My mother read the war news every day.
She worried a lot. I didn't know what to do for her.

When we went to the movies,
we saw newsreels of the war.

There was scary music, and a dramatic voice
saying things like: "Enemy forces stagger under
the powerful punch of U.S. air power. . . ."

An admiral came to town and told us
how we would win the war.

The admiral was Denny Rankin's
mother's cousin, and Denny got
to stand next to him afterward.

We couldn't
understand
how a brat
like Denny
could have
an admiral
for a relative.

Winter came, and one day we got
a letter from my father.
He had been sent to Florida
to run some hotels
for the army.

He said we should come down to
Florida during school vacation.

HOT DOG !
HOT DIGGETY
DOG !!

It took three days.
The train was packed
with soldiers and sailors.

We were lucky. We got berths in the sleeping car.
I climbed a ladder to my berth.
Once you were in your berth, you closed
the curtains and snapped them shut.

Then you had to get out of your clothes
and into your pajamas.
After that you could watch the towns go by.

At last we got to Florida, and got off the train . . .

and there was my father.

My father took me to where he worked.
Soldiers saluted him. I was very proud.

We went swimming in the ocean
on Christmas day. It was warm.

We went sight-seeing.
My parents loved seeing flamingos.
I didn't mind one or two.

There were a lot of things
I thought we should see.
My parents didn't think so.

Then it was time for us to leave. We went to the airport.

"When will you come home?" I said.

"As soon as the war's over," said my father.

That sounded like practically never to me.

Back home the war
went on and on.

The tinfoil I collected
got as big as a bowling ball.

We stopped putting out *The Blackout*
when Sally Ann Curtis's brother got killed in Germany.
We didn't know what to say.

One day I heard cars honking and
bells ringing and whistles blowing.
I rode my bike to the center of town.

Old Mr. Murphy was standing
in the street, waving his hat
and cane.

"What's going on, Mr. Murphy?"
I asked.
"Don't you know the war is over?"
he cried. "We won, we won!"

Three weeks later my brother came home.
A month after that all three of us
were at the station to meet my father.
He saw us, and he waved.

That's when I knew the war was over.